THREE VOTES

David_mcmli

Paperback: 978-1-968667-03-0
eBook: 978-1-968667-04-7
Library of Congress Control Number: 2025913163

This is a work of fiction.

Ordering Information:

Prime Seven Media
518 Landmann St.
Tomah City, WI 54660

Printed in the United States of America

Table of Contents

CHAPTER 1

The Envelope

*E*lliot Kane didn't so much retire from football as drift away from it, like a shadow fading under floodlights. A decade in the system — 187 games, 47 goals, and not a single season where he felt like he truly belonged. He was good enough to play, never quite great enough to be remembered.

He walked away after Round 22 of his final season with no press conference, no farewell lap, no retrospective package. His manager released a single sentence: *"Elliot Kane will pursue other opportunities outside football."* What that really meant was: he'd had enough. Enough of the manipulation. Enough of the closed-door conversations. Enough of being a chess piece on someone else's board.

He wasn't bitter. He was done.

Post-footy, he disappeared into delivery work — literal deliveries. Confidential couriers. Government contracts. A man with a license, a clean record, and no reason to be noticed. It suited him. He liked the silence. No one asked for autographs. No one asked why he didn't quite become the star the junior scouts had promised. There were no performance reviews, no match committees. Just him, a van, and the voice of Brad Hardies talkback radio crackling through the console.

And in that silence, something in Elliot began to wake — the part of him that had always been watching, storing, questioning. Not just about football, but about power. About the machinery behind the scoreboard. The strange conversations after matches. The look in the coach's eyes before a mid-season game where he was suddenly omitted without explanation. The club exec who once said, *"You'll thank us for this in five years."* But five years came. And Elliot didn't thank them.

By the time the envelope arrived — thick, sealed, unsigned — Elliot Kane was no longer just a former player.

He was something else entirely: a man ready to ask what everyone else had trained themselves never to say aloud.

And this time, he wouldn't be part of the game.

He would investigate it.

CHAPTER 2

The Delivery to Rennick

*E*lliot Kane parked the motorbike outside AFL House just before 9 a.m., his black courier jacket zipped up against the Melbourne wind and his helmet visor streaked with dry city grit. He unclipped the leather satchel from his back and pulled out a single envelope — heavy stock, sealed with black wax, no name, no return address.

Just a single phrase in ink on the front:

"To David Rennick — Confidential."

He read the name again. Rennick.

David Rennick.

There weren't many names that could still sour Elliot's stomach. But that one? That one was different.

He hadn't spoken to Rennick since 2011 — the year Elliot finished equal second in the Brownlow count and still somehow didn't win. Thirty-five touches in Round 22, two goals, five clearances in the last quarter. Everyone said it was his moment.

But on the night?

"Three votes... to number 24... from Carlton."

Wrong team. Wrong player. Wrong everything.

Elliot hadn't asked questions at the time. You don't question the system. You thank it for remembering you at all.

But later that year, when he was recovering from a torn calf and trying to sort contract extensions, he saw it.

Rennick — then at Carlton — having drinks at a function with the umpire from that final round. Laughing like old mates. No big deal, people said. Everyone knows everyone in footy.

Except Elliot didn't.

He'd raised it once, carefully, with his player manager.

"Drop it," he was told. "You sound paranoid."

So he did. Publicly. Professionally.

But privately? He remembered.

And when Rennick got promoted to the AFL executive ranks two years later — Head of Integrity — Elliot almost choked.

That word. Integrity.

It stirred something deep. David Rennick — former club director turned AFL executive, head of

"Game Integrity & Values," whatever that meant these days. Elliot hadn't seen him since the night he lost the Brownlow by three votes.

Not that he cared. Not anymore.

He took the elevator up, watching his reflection bounce across the brushed metal walls — a man once known for gut-running and clean hands now delivering envelopes for a living. He didn't look like a footballer anymore. But he still walked like one — upright, like he hadn't learned how to quit.

The receptionist at Level 10 wore the kind of neutral smile reserved for former players.

"Delivery for Mr Rennick," Elliot said, placing the envelope on the counter.

She reached out automatically, then hesitated.

"Do you have ID for the sender?"

"No name," Elliot replied. "It came through the dispatch hub this morning. No signature. Just 'hand to Rennick directly.'"

She frowned. "I'll see if he's available."

Before she could pick up the phone, a voice rang out from the glass-walled office to the right.

"It's alright. He can come in."

Rennick himself. Wearing a navy suit, white shirt, no tie. Still lean, still too smooth. He smiled like a man who'd never been found guilty of anything.

Elliot stepped inside the office and set the envelope on the desk.

"Didn't expect to see you again," Rennick said, not looking up.

"Same."

They stood in silence a beat too long.

"You are working for one of the courier mobs now?"

"Independents," Elliot replied. "Pays better."

Rennick raised an eyebrow. "Still bitter?"

Elliot almost laughed. "Still standing."

Rennick picked up the envelope, weighing it in his hand.

"Anything else?"

"Nope."

Elliot turned and left, but not before catching a glimpse of something strange.

A man standing just beyond the next office window — dressed like club staff but unfamiliar. Heavy build. Neatly trimmed beard. Sunglasses on his cap. Watching him too intently.

By the time Elliot reached the elevator, he couldn't stop replaying the moment. Something about it sat wrong. Not threatening — just… out of place.

Down in the car park, he slid on his helmet, started the bike, and told himself to forget it.

But halfway across the city, he pulled over. Something kept itching at the base of his neck.

He called the one person who never ignored him.

Tash answered on the first ring. "Tell me it's not weird again."

"It's weird."

"What happened?"

"I just delivered a envelope to David Rennick."

"So?"

"So, someone in that office wasn't supposed to be there. And I've got a feeling... this delivery wasn't just mail."

Now here he was, nearly a decade later, delivering a envelope to the same man, and catching a glimpse of a stranger watching the handoff like it meant something.

Coincidence? Maybe.

But Elliot had played long enough to know one truth:

In footy, coincidences don't wear suits.

Elliot had a personal flashback interlude expanding the deep, bitter history between him and David Rennick. This dives into Elliot's internal scars, the politics that shaped his fall, and the betrayal he never voiced — until now.

The thing about betrayal, Elliot had learned, is that it doesn't always come with a knife.

Sometimes it comes with a handshake and a microphone.

Brownlow Night, 2011.

He'd worn a charcoal suit and a cautious smile. Not the favourite, not the showman — but the workhorse. The one who'd earned it the hard way. He'd polled well all year. Carried a team going nowhere. Laid more tackles than half the leaderboard combined.

Round 22 was his masterpiece. A final statement. One last plea to the gods of memory.

But when the count hit Round 22, the room shifted. It always did — that strange hush before someone's life changed.

Elliot sat, hands folded, heart not racing but listening.

"One vote... Carlton."

"Two votes... Essendon."

"Three votes... Carlton."

His name never came.

He'd stared straight ahead, unmoving. Heard the applause. Saw the winner rise. Smiled for the camera.

But in his chest, something tore quietly.

Three days later, he was at a club sponsor luncheon, wearing a bandage on his calf and fielding questions about free agency. That's when he saw them — Rennick and the umpire from Round 22. Laughing. Elbows on the bar. Two drinks deep.

He told himself it meant nothing.

But Rennick had only just left his role as a club director. Still had influence. Still had reach. And Elliot knew what that laugh sounded like — the one you saved for when you'd played a good hand behind closed doors.

Elliot never accused him. Never even asked. That's not how it worked.

But something shifted.

A week later, his contract offer was quietly downgraded.

Six months later, he was delisted.

One year after that, Rennick was working at AFL House.

The man who had helped remove him from the game now sat in charge of "game integrity."

Elliot never said a word. But he remembered every vote. Every nod. Every silence.

And now, after all this time, he was delivering an unmarked envelope to that same man... and watching a ghost in a green bib linger in the shadows behind him.

It wasn't just unfinished business anymore.

It was open season.

CHAPTER 3

The Man in the Bib

Tash Pearson didn't follow football. She followed patterns. Data, algorithms, footage anomalies, human glitches. In her world, everything had a signal — even silence.

Elliot stood behind her as she replayed the footage he'd found. A background camera feed from the Level 10 foyer, pulled from a secure server using credentials she technically no longer had access to.

She zoomed in. There he was.

The man.

Same beard. Same sunglasses perched on a navy cap. This time wearing a green staff bib with a club logo half-folded over. He wasn't just watching Elliot — he was timed to his arrival.

"He was already inside before you got there," Tash muttered, "but not in any security log. I've run three matchday databases, AFL staff lists, even the post-COVID accreditation archives. Nothing."

"So, what is he?" Elliot asked.

"Best guess? Ghost access. Given a bib and a name that isn't his."

Elliot exhaled slowly. "Someone made sure he looked like he belonged."

"Or," Tash added, "someone wanted him to be seen by you."

That stopped Elliot. He didn't like being part of someone else's setup. He'd been set up before — the 'clean hands' guy told to smile on camera while the club board bartered behind closed doors.

Tash clicked through her keyboard with the rhythm of someone halfway to the truth. Then paused.

"Found something."

She pulled up a still image from a match three weeks earlier. Saints v Hawks. A player limped off. Trainers jogged on.

And behind them — just for a moment — the same man. Standing inside the boundary line, speaking to an umpire.

"You see that?" she said. "He's talking to the ump. On field. No med kit. No water."

Elliot leaned in. "He doesn't even move like a trainer. He's waiting."

"I've got his face clean this time," she said, capturing the still. "Cross-reference in progress."

Seconds passed. Then: MATCH FOUND –
VINCENT MARINO.

The screen filled with old news clippings. Alleged
links to betting syndicates. Guest lists for charity balls.
No convictions, just whispers. Mostly dismissed as
tabloid speculation.

One headline stood out.

"THE SHADOW SPONSOR: AFL's Silent Backer
with a Shady Past"

And the subheading:

> "Vincent Marino's business interests
> include hospitality groups, crypto wallets
> — and a stake in three major sports betting
> apps."

Tash sat back. "So why is he dressed like a trainer?"

Elliot didn't answer right away. His eyes hadn't left
the image.

"I played in a match once," he said slowly. "Late in
the season. We were out of finals contention, but I was
flying. Had 30 at half time. The votes should've been
mine, easily."

"What happened?"

"We lost. I didn't poll a vote."

"Normal?"

"No. But I figured it was just the way the game goes."

"And now?"

"Now I wonder if someone made sure of it."

They sat in silence, the hum of the laptop the only sound in the room.

Then Tash spoke again. "We need someone who's been around the league longer than us. Someone who's seen this kind of smoke before."

Elliot didn't hesitate.

"Call Brad Hardie."

CHAPTER 4

The Medallist Speaks

*B*rad Hardie still did radio the old-fashioned way — in a dusty corner studio filled with reel-to-reel tapes, Carlton Draft memorabilia, and the smell of stale coffee and leather-bound stat sheets.

The Brownlow Medallist turned broadcaster didn't do filters, didn't do favours, and didn't owe the AFL a damn thing.

Which is why Elliot trusted him.

They met after-hours at the community radio station where Brad still did his weekly show, Hard Truths. He greeted Elliot with a rough handshake and a raised eyebrow.

"Well, look what the dog dragged in," Brad said, half-smiling. "Last time I saw you, you were limping off the MCG and swearing at a boot."

"Some things haven't changed," Elliot replied.

Brad led him to the studio's back room, where an old kettle wheezed and a whiteboard still had match notes from the 2006 prelim final.

Tash joined them via video call, her voice crackling through an ageing speaker.

Elliot got straight to the point.

"Have you ever heard of Vincent Marino?"

Brad's face didn't change, but something in his eyes hardened.

"I've heard about him. Enough to stay out of his way."

"We found footage of him dressed as a club trainer," Elliot said. "On the field. Talking to umpires. No accreditation."

Brad nodded slowly. "Sounds about right. Heard whispers years ago that he was backing clubs through shell sponsorships. Box seats. Corporate deals. Never proved."

"Could he influence votes?" Tash asked.

Brad leaned back. "If you're asking if votes can be influenced — yes. Have been for decades. Umpires are human. They're not corrupt, most of them — they're just… suggestible. They hear narratives, read headlines. A word here, a nod there. It doesn't take much."

"And Marino?"

Brad sighed. "He's got interests in betting markets from Singapore to Malta. I heard he once flew a group of boundary umpires to a private resort in Bali for 'wellness training.' AFL turned a blind eye."

Elliot clenched his fists. "Why?"

"Because he's also backed three major club redevelopment projects. Half the league's execs owe him a favour."

Tash's voice cut in. "We think he's not just influencing results — he's selecting winners. Engineering a Brownlow outcome."

Brad's laugh was short and dry. "Wouldn't shock me. The Brownlow's a brand now, not a medal. Big money rides on the votes. Exotic bets. Fantasy leagues. International markets."

Elliot leaned forward. "Would you go public?"

Brad didn't flinch.

"I've been itching to burn that place down for years. But if I do it alone, I'm just a bitter old has-been. If you two have proof, then I'll shout it from the rooftops."

He picked up a notepad and scratched out a name.

"Start with Mick Dalley. Former umpire. Clean as they come — until he wasn't. Quietly resigned last year. No injury. No scandal. Just gone. He'll talk, if someone gives him a reason."

Tash nodded. "We'll find him."

Brad's eyes narrowed. "Just be careful. If Marino's involved, this isn't just about footy. It's about money. Real money. The kind people kill over."

Elliot stood, thanked him, and walked out into the cool Melbourne night.

He could feel it now — the shift.

This wasn't about his vote anymore.

It was about all of them.

Updated saved memory

Understood — from here on, each chapter of Three Votes will escalate with tension, unexpected revelations, and moral complexity. Twists won't just shock — they'll deepen the conspiracy, complicate alliances, and keep the reader guessing.

CHAPTER 5

The Whistle That Wasn't Blown

Mick Dalley lived in a rented weatherboard house two hours out of Melbourne; off a road Google Maps didn't bother naming. Elliot and Tash arrived just before sundown, headlights bouncing off rusted gates and overgrown bushland.

Dalley answered the door in thongs and a faded cricket tee. He looked thinner than his old umpiring photos — older, like someone who'd seen too much and said too little for too long.

"I know who you are," he said to Elliot. "And I know why you're here."

Tash held up a printout — the still frame of Marino speaking to the umpire. "We just need to know what this is."

Dalley didn't invite them in. He pointed to a bench on the porch, sat down himself, and lit a cigarette with fingers that trembled slightly.

"I walked away for a reason," he muttered. "And it wasn't injury or family. It was this."

Elliot stayed silent. Let him speak.

Dalley exhaled. "There's a list."

"A list?" Tash asked.

Dalley nodded. "Every season, somewhere around Round 14, we'd get a file. Internal guidance, they called it. Nothing official. Just 'contextual notes.' Said it helped keep consistency."

"What was in it?" Elliot asked.

"Player trends. Club narratives. Umpire rotation history. But also… suggestions. Highlighted names. Momentum guys. 'Keep an eye on.' At first, I thought it was marketing stuff. PR-friendly. Then I saw something strange."

He pulled out a battered folder and unzipped it. Inside, a single laminated page.

It looked harmless — just a spreadsheet.

But the columns were labelled:

- Player Name
- Match Round
- Suggested Points
- Rationale
- Betting Exposure

Tash's eyes widened. "Betting exposure?"

Dalley tapped the page. "That's when I knew. It wasn't about performance anymore. It was about positioning."

"Where did this come from?" Elliot asked.

Dalley shook his head. "It was left in my umpire locker by mistake. Meant for someone else, I think. No initials. No stamp. Just a red tag in the corner. I kept it. Made a copy. The original disappeared the next day."

Tash studied the names. One jumped out.

J. Matheson – Round 18 – 3 votes – rationale: bounce back narrative, high fan sentiment.

"But he barely touched it that round," Elliot said.

Dalley nodded. "Didn't matter. He was marketable. Rising star. Big club. The sponsors wanted a headline."

"And Marino?"

Dalley's voice lowered. "He's never named. But I saw him once. After a game, back of house. Not on the books but shaking hands with the senior umpire manager.

Just once. I asked who he was — got told he was a 'corporate advisor.' Next week, I was rotated out of primetime games."

Elliot leaned forward. "Why didn't you go public?"

Dalley crushed his cigarette into the timber. "You ever heard what happened to Liam Gray?"

Tash paused. "The junior timekeeper who got 'robbed' in Southbank?"

Dalley looked them dead in the eye. "He told his brother he was going to leak match audio. Said it didn't line up with the final report. Two nights later, he's in hospital. No one charged. Just a 'random' attack."

Elliot's chest tightened. "You think it was connected?"

"I know it was."

Dalley stood. "You're playing with a rigged deck. These people don't care about sport. They care about odds. About perception. About money so big it moves governments."

He walked back to the door.

"I kept quiet because I didn't want to be next. But you two? If you're already in… don't stop halfway."

Then he looked directly at Elliot.

"You were robbed once. Don't let them rob everyone else."

The door closed behind him.

Tash turned to Elliot. "This isn't a leak anymore. It's a war."

CHAPTER 6

The Pattern

Jash didn't sleep.

While Elliot replayed Dalley's words and tried not to spiral, she fed every Brownlow vote from the past three seasons into her custom analytics engine — a machine she called Fitzroy, after a club the league let die without blinking.

She cross-referenced votes with historical betting data scraped from dozens of public and grey-market sources, then filtered for anomalies: Brownlow night betting spikes, sudden line movements, exotic multis, and irregular market shifts in the days leading up to the vote count.

By dawn, she had it.

A name.

Tyson Colville.

Midfielder. Played for a mid-table club that hadn't made the finals in five years. Talented, but not flashy. Finished fourth in last year's Brownlow — a good story, a surprise to most. But the numbers said otherwise.

"Colville was barely on the radar mid-season," Tash explained over coffee. "Then three days before the Brownlow, massive bets started pouring in — not just on him to finish top 5, but in exact finishing order multis. Tens of thousands placed through obscure overseas books."

Elliot leaned in. "So, someone knew?"

"Someone didn't just know," she said. "They published it. Across three separate platforms, the same bet appeared: Colville to finish fourth, behind three predictable favourites — in exact order."

She flipped her laptop around. Betting slips. Payout receipts. Forum posts timestamped two nights before the Brownlow count.

"And here's the kicker," she added. "All of them were made through accounts tied to shell companies — and those companies? They trace back to betting exchanges Marino has holdings in."

Elliot stared at the screen. "So, it's not just match influence... it's endgame rigging."

Tash nodded. "They don't bet round-by-round. They wait until the votes are final, sealed, but not yet announced. And someone inside leaks them. Or worse — someone inside writes them."

"They're betting like it's a closed race," Elliot said. "Because it is."

She nodded again. "It's like knowing the Melbourne Cup result before it's run — and only placing your bets in the last furlong."

"And the AFL?"

"They have the access logs. They just don't want the questions."

Later that day, Brad Hardie called.

"I've had a whisper," he said quietly. "Someone high up in AFL Comms tried to spike a story last year. A journo was working on a piece tied to Brownlow week betting. Got shut down. Cold."

"Do you know the journo?" Elliot asked.

"I do," Brad replied. "And she's been waiting for someone like you to knock on her door."

He gave them a name.

Cleo Watson. Former sportswriter. Now freelance. Reputation for truth. Reputation for not playing nice with the AFL.

Elliot stood, pulse quickening. "Let's go."

Tash grabbed her keys. "If the game is rigged, we need someone who's already tried to blow the whistle."

"And this time," Elliot said, "we won't let them silence her."

CHAPTER 7

Cleo's Silence

*C*leo Watson met them at a Brunswick café where no one ordered skinny lattes and the cutlery came in mason jars. She wore mirrored sunglasses, a denim jacket, and the tension of someone who'd been hunted but never caught.

"I'm only talking because Brad said you're real," she said, motioning them to sit. "One minute. If I don't like your questions, I walk."

Elliot leaned forward. "You were working on a Brownlow betting story last year."

Her lips twitched — not a smile. A warning.

"I was working on a dozen stories. That's how it works. You pitch a dozen. They kill the one that's too close."

Tash pulled a betting slip and photo from her folder — the one tying Tyson Colville's exact Brownlow finish to a shell company with ties to Vincent Marino.

Cleo didn't even flinch. "I know the slip. I know the name. But I couldn't publish it."

"Why?" Tash asked.

"Because the AFL's lawyers rang the paper before I even filed. Told the editor I was planning to 'undermine the integrity of the game.'"

"Were you?" Elliot asked.

"I was trying to save it," she snapped. "But they didn't care. They only care about optics. Integrity is their brand, not their practice."

She sipped her coffee and pulled out a phone. Opened her notes app. Swiped through dozens of headlines — all killed.

"The Hidden Odds: How the Brownlow Became a Betting Market's Playground."

"Off the Record: The AFL's Undeclared Corporate 'Supporters.'"

"Beyond the White Line: Trainers, Umpires, and the Silence in Between."

"They shut me down. But worse — they offered me something else."

Elliot frowned. "What?"

"A consulting gig. Media liaison with AFL Media's in-house arm. Said I'd be 'perfect to help shape the narrative.'"

"Buyout," Tash muttered.

Cleo nodded. "Polite blackmail. Say no, lose access. Say yes, lose your soul."

She paused. The café hummed around them. Outside, a tram rattled past.

"I kept everything. Sources, contacts, transcripts. But if I release it, I'll be sued to death. They don't need to win — they just need to exhaust me."

Tash leaned in. "What if we gave you new proof? Tied to Dalley, to leaked access logs, to someone on the inside feeding votes before Brownlow night?"

Cleo's voice dropped.

"Then I publish. Independent. Full expose. But I need one more thing."

"What?" Elliot asked.

"A face. Someone in the machine. Someone who knew it and helped it happen."

Tash's eyes narrowed. "A whistleblower."

"Exactly."

Cleo stood, tossed a ten-dollar note on the table.

"You bring me that, and I'll bring the league to its knees."

CHAPTER 8

The Weight They Carried

They found him in a rehab clinic on the outskirts of Geelong. No cameras. No press releases. Just a false name on the register and a face that once lit up the MCG in September.

Dale Reardon.

Dual club best and fairest. All-Australian midfielder. Retired suddenly at 29 "for personal reasons." No farewell game. No lap of honour.

Elliot hadn't spoken to him in years.

But now, he sat beside Reardon on a wooden bench in the clinic's quiet garden, surrounded by recovering addicts and forgotten promises. Dale looked thinner. Greyer. Not in body — in spirit.

"You here to write a book?" Dale asked.

"No," Elliot replied. "I'm here because something's broken. And I think you were one of the first to feel it."

Dale didn't answer at first. Just stared at the trembling leaves of a gum tree.

"I knew I wasn't going to win the Brownlow," he said eventually. "But I also knew I was polling. Coaches told me. Teammates. The media. Then the night comes... and nothing. Not a vote."

Elliot nodded slowly. "Same happened to me."

"It wasn't just ego," Dale said. "It was what it did to me. You train your whole life to be elite — and then the game tells you, you're invisible. And you believe it."

He rubbed his hands, knuckles cracked and raw.

"I started pushing harder. Playing hurt. Taking risks. Trying to 'be seen.' Started hearing whispers that I didn't 'fit the AFL's image.' No media polish. No sponsor smile. Just a ball-winner."

Tash stepped forward. "Did you ever suspect something more?"

"I didn't want to. Because if it's rigged, then every injury, every sacrifice, every fan you let down — it's for nothing."

He looked at Elliot.

"I broke ribs in a dead rubber game because I thought one more clearance might get me noticed. Instead, the votes went to a bloke who had twelve touches and one TV ad."

Tears formed in the corners of his eyes but didn't fall.

"The painkillers stopped working. So, I moved on to something stronger."

Elliot sat in silence. He understood now that this wasn't just about money or titles. This was about identity theft. About the system quietly dismantling the souls of the men it used.

"I have names," Dale whispered. "Guys who got calls from 'advisors' — telling them to play 'media-friendly.' Coaches told to 'rest' certain players so others could shine."

"Would you talk to the press?" Tash asked.

Dale hesitated. Then shook his head.

"Not yet. But I'll give you a name. Someone who is still inside. Someone who hears the whispers from behind closed doors."

He handed them a note.

A name scribbled in black ink.

Jordan Elsey — AFL Match Operations, Compliance Analyst.

"Find him," Dale said. "And tell him I sent you."

Elliot stood. "Are you okay?"

Dale looked at him — honestly, painfully.

"No. But I will be, if someone finally tells the truth."

CHAPTER 9

The Man Behind the Curtain

Jordan Elsey worked out of AFL House — level 7, Compliance and Match Operations. A man no one noticed. Which made him perfect.

Elliot had seen him before in passing, years ago — during tribunal hearings, club briefings, injury disclosures. He had the look of someone who watched everything and said nothing. Quiet shoes. Crisp notes. A whisperer with access.

Tash tracked his schedule via a private LinkedIn scrape and an old staff rota archived online. Thursday. 3:10 PM. Logistics briefing, Docklands Stadium.

Elliot waited outside the elevator shaft.

When Elsey emerged, lanyard swinging and phone in hand, Elliot stepped in quietly beside him.

"Jordan. I need a word."

Elsey blinked. "Elliot Kane?"

"In the flesh."

"I didn't know you were still… involved."

"I wasn't. Now I am."

He nodded slowly. "You shouldn't be here."

"I know. That's why I'm here."

They sat on a concrete bench beside the stadium's loading dock. Nearby, crew moved crates of signage and goalpost pads. Trucks rumbled. Wind carried the scent of stale pies and broadcast cables.

"I've been told you know things," Elliot said.

"I know systems," Elsey replied. "Not people."

"Systems are built by people," Tash added, appearing from behind the ramp.

Jordan didn't flinch. He looked from one to the other, measured them, then sighed.

"I assume this is about votes."

"And betting," Elliot said.

"And Marino," Tash finished.

Elsey paused — just long enough to say everything without words.

"You're not wrong," he said. "But you're not ready, either. Because once you go past theory, once you have names, proof, evidence… then you have enemies."

"We already do," Elliot said.

"Not like this," Elsey said. "You think you're uncovering a scandal? You're poking at a machine. This thing funds stadiums. Pays TV salaries. Keeps clubs' solvent. Betting dollars are baked into the code."

"Do you have anything?" Tash asked.

Jordan opened his tablet, turned the screen toward them.

A graph.

"Internal server logs from the week before last year's Brownlow," he explained. "Between Monday night and Wednesday morning, six unauthorized logins to the umpire review database — from a device not registered to the AFL. No audit trail. No trace. But a packet dump shows the files accessed."

He swiped.

A document appeared. Titled:

> "Brownlow Voting Master list – Final Draft
> – For Internal Preview Only"

Timestamped five days before the count.

"This is how they do it," Jordan said. "The votes are 'finalised' days out. Not just tallied — packaged. Branded. Previewed by certain corporate partners. Once that doc exists, it can be sold."

Tash screenshot it. "Can you leak this?"

"I can't," Jordan said. "Not without risking my family."

"But you have," Elliot said.

Jordan looked down. "Not to you."

He stood.

"One more thing," he said. "Be careful around Cleo Watson. She's not the only one listening to your investigation. Someone's tracking her too."

Elliot frowned. "Who?"

But Jordan was already walking away.

That night, back at Tash's apartment, the mood was heavy.

Elliot stared at the wall. Tash tapped endlessly through encryption protocols. Cleo wasn't answering her phone.

Then it rang.

A private number. Elliot answered.

A male voice. Flat. Distant.

"Cleo Watson has been in an accident. Inner-city bike collision. Fatal injuries. Police investigating."

Silence.

Tash covered her mouth. Elliot closed his eyes.

"No further information will be provided," the voice added. "Thank you."

Click.

The line went dead.

CHAPTER 10

The Ripple and the Rage

*C*leo's death hit harder than either of them expected. Elliot hadn't known her long, but something about her fierce independence had made her feel permanent — like a stake in the ground of truth. Now she was gone. A cyclist hit by a delivery truck. No CCTV. No witnesses. Police ruled it an accident before breakfast.

Tash didn't cry. She typed.

She poured over the final messages Cleo had sent. Half-written article drafts. Audio memos. One file stood out. A voice recording, time-stamped two hours before she died.

"If anything happens to me, know this: someone inside knows. There's a script — a template — and the votes follow it. This isn't theory anymore. It's choreography."

Then static.

Then silence.

Tash replayed it five times before she let it go.

Elliot stayed quiet most of the day. He didn't speak until the sun was nearly down and the glow of the city blinked through the apartment's blinds.

"She knew the risks," he said finally.

"That doesn't make it right," Tash replied.

"I didn't say it did."

She turned. "So, what now? We back off. Pretend this never happened? Let someone else die next time?"

Elliot looked at her — really looked.

Tash stood like a blade: sharp, tense, forged by purpose. But there was a tremble in her voice, and a fatigue behind her eyes that no algorithm could mask.

He stepped closer. "We don't back off. But we don't charge forward blind either."

"And Cleo?"

"She gets the story. We finish what she started."

There was a pause between them. Charged. Wordless.

Tash broke it with a breath. "You know I used to hate this game?"

"Footy?"

"Yeah. Thought it was stupid. A way to distract people from asking real questions."

"And now?"

"Now I know it's the perfect place to hide answers."

He almost smiled — almost. Instead, he looked down, and when he looked back up, something in him had softened.

"I'm glad you're in this with me," he said quietly.

"So am I."

A long silence. Not uncomfortable. Just there.

Then a knock at the door.

Tash walked cautiously to it and checked the peephole. No one.

She opened it slowly.

An envelope lay on the ground.

Inside: a photo.

A man in a pub, mid-conversation — gesturing emphatically to someone off-frame.

On the back, a note:

> "Your next vote-rigger. His name's Raff Deluca. He's closer than you think."

CHAPTER 11

Deluca's Deal

Raff Deluca didn't work for the AFL. He worked around it — a smooth operator with too many phones and no public job title. Officially, he was listed as a "Commercial Engagement Liaison" for a boutique marketing agency in Richmond.

Unofficially, he made things happen.

Elliot remembered his name from years ago — mostly whispered in players' lounges and pub corners. The guy who could get you a sponsor, smooth out a minor tribunal charge, help your club win favour with the fixture schedulers. Always one step removed, never in the press.

Tash tracked him using facial-recognition overlays from the pub photo. Within two hours, they had a pattern: Deluca met with club executives before key matches, usually in quiet venues. He moved between multiple stadium zones on match day — never staying long enough to be official, always with the right lanyard.

"He's got a network," Tash muttered. "Mid-level club staff, retired players, fringe agents. All moving quietly."

"And votes?" Elliot asked.

She nodded. "We think he preps them."

Elliot raised an eyebrow.

Tash brought up a document on her screen. "Not the actual 3-2-1s. But the conditions. He crafts the storyline — feeds talking points to broadcasters, prompts radio callers, drops whispers to coaches."

"Shaping perception," Elliot said.

"Exactly. By the time the umpires review the footage, the narratives already built — who starred, who turned the match, who had the 'moment.' And if you control the moment…"

"You control the votes."

Tash nodded grimly.

They needed proof. So, they followed him.

Friday night. Marvel Stadium. Deluca arrived two hours before bounce-down with a bag slung over his shoulder and an access pass borrowed from a sponsor's rep. Tash tracked his movements using signal triangulation from a burner device Elliot carried in his back pocket.

He stopped for a quiet meeting with a club welfare officer.

Then with a local radio producer.

Then, finally, in a VIP suite — where they saw him hand over a file folder to a man Elliot recognized immediately:

Nevin Kay — the AFL's Head of Strategic Media.

Tash snapped a photo through the glass.

"I knew Kay back in the day," Elliot muttered. "Used to be clean. Spoke at school clinics. Now he's briefing media on who should poll before the game even starts."

As they backed away from the window, Elliot's phone buzzed.

An unknown number. Text only:

"Stop watching. Or start running."

Then, a second message. This time a photo.
Of Tash.
Taken from behind as she stood in front of her apartment block.

Elliot's stomach dropped. He looked at Tash — who was already going pale.

"They know," she whispered.

And for the first time, Elliot saw something in her he hadn't before.

Fear.

Real fear.

He reached for her hand. Didn't think — just did it.

"I'm not letting anything happen to you," he said.

She didn't let go.

The Puppet Master

Nevin Kay was polished. Ex-sports journo turned AFL media strategist. Hair slicked, tie neat, voice always two tones below suspicion. He was the kind of man who smiled at funerals if the cameras were rolling.

Elliot and Tash waited for him outside a café near Southbank. He liked to meet influencers there. Kay treated journos like children, players like currency, and narratives like chess pieces. He was always ten moves ahead — until now.

He clocked them from across the footpath. Didn't flinch. Just walked up, latte in hand.

"I assume this isn't catch-up."

"You've seen the footage," Elliot said flatly. "You took a file from Deluca."

Kay didn't blink. "You'll need to be more specific."

"Don't bother lying," Tash added. "We've got the photo. We've also got a timestamp, an angle, and a witness who saw you brief two media personnel before the match."

Kay sipped his latte. "Media runs on prep. You don't brief them, they speculate. You want chaos?"

"We want truth," Elliot snapped.

"Then publish it," Kay shrugged. "Leak it. Make a noise. But understand this — you think you're uncovering a scandal. What you're actually doing is threatening a billion-dollar industry built on perception."

"Built on lies," Tash corrected.

Kay's gaze hardened.

"No. Built on hope. People need stars. Heroes. Redemption arcs. If we leave it to reality, we get mud-stained midfielders who mumble and can't sell toothpaste. You want the truth? No one watches that."

He stepped closer.

"Votes aren't 'rigged.' They're… curated. Steered. The umpires are human — we just offer them context."

"Context?" Elliot said, rising. "You script results."

Kay dropped his smile.

"You're old news, Kane. A cautionary tale. You could've been a legend, but you weren't marketable. So you got nothing. That's the game."

Silence fell like a dropped guillotine.

Then Tash stood.

"People are dying. Cleo. Maybe others. Your part of this — even if you don't get your hands dirty."

Kay turned to leave. "Careful. That sort of talk? It gets you dropped from more than just guest lists."

As he walked off, Elliot noticed a car parked across the street — the same one they'd seen two nights in a row outside Tash's apartment. A black sedan, engine running, driver never stepping out.

They were being followed.

And Nevin knew it.

Back at the apartment, Tash double-encrypted their files and moved everything onto multiple drives.

"From now on," she said, "we don't meet in the open. We don't talk on phones. And we trust no one."

Elliot looked out the window. The car was gone.

But the feeling wasn't.

CHAPTER 13

The Whistle That Never Blew

They found him living in Ballarat, in a weathered red-brick cottage behind a crumbling fence. The kind of place where footy jerseys were framed in back rooms and nothing got thrown out unless it had truly given up.

Ronnie Tilton.

Former AFL umpire. 234 games. Known for his calm presence and sharp eyes. Retired suddenly in 2013 without explanation. The papers called it "timing." He called it "enough."

Ronnie opened the door in a cardigan and slippers. Looked Elliot up and down.

"I remember you. Carlton. Left footer. Smart with the ball."

Elliot nodded. "You gave me a few frees."

Ronnie smiled faintly. "Only when you earned 'em."

They sat in his lounge room, surrounded by silence and the scent of liniment that never quite left his life. A mantle held old match balls, a crinkled photo of him shaking hands with Glenn Archer, and a worn Bible.

"I heard about Cleo," Ronnie said softly. "She came to me last year. Asked questions. I didn't answer them. I was afraid."

Tash said nothing, just listened.

"I wasn't paid off. Not directly. No brown paper bags, no threats. But you get… nudged. Encouraged. Before games, there'd be chats. 'This bloke had a big week in the media, might've earned a look.' Or 'We want the game to breathe — don't ping the stars early.' It sounds innocent."

"But it builds," Elliot said.

Ronnie looked at the fire. "It does. Then one day you're watching a kid get scragged all game, and you let it go. Because the script's already been written — and you're just a prop man."

He reached for a folder on the coffee table. "I kept this. Never knew why."

Inside were pages of handwritten notes — game logs, whistle codes, instructions he'd been given from a "comms director" before key matches.

One note stood out:

"Round 19 – Prime Time – Watch for #9 (Colville). Narrative: comeback hero. Give room. He's polling."

Tash's eyes flicked up. "They told you he was polling?"

Ronnie shook his head. "Not directly. But it was always implied. 'He's the story tonight.' That was the phrase."

"And what did you do?" Elliot asked.

"I swallowed it. Like I'd swallowed a hundred others. But that one stuck. I knew I'd lost something that night."

He stood, walked slowly to a dusty bookshelf, and pulled out an unopened envelope. Handed it to Elliot.

"This was sent to me three years ago. No return address. Inside, there's a list of Brownlow top threes from each round — all correct. All before the count."

Elliot opened it carefully. The paper was yellowing. The names lined up like a graveyard of forgotten truth.

"Why didn't you go to the media?" Tash asked.

Ronnie looked down.

"Because I thought the game would fix itself. Because I was tired. Because I was ashamed."

A long silence settled.

Then he looked up, eyes wet.

"Don't make the same mistake. Tell the truth — even if no one listens."

Elliot gripped his hand firmly.

"We will."

CHAPTER 14

The Breach

Jash didn't sleep for two nights. She stayed up scanning metadata logs, rerouting proxy filters, hunting for shadows in AFL House's digital basement.

On the third night, she found it.

A breach.

Small, surgical — just five minutes of access in a back-end server marked "AFL-Vote Integrity Archive." Not public. Not indexed. Password protected behind four walls of corporate firewalls.

Someone had used an internal access credential to download the sealed Brownlow vote ledger three days before last year's count. The IP address was masked — mostly. But not perfectly.

The source? A secure device assigned to Daniel Kreel, head of AFL data governance.

Elliot knew the name.

"He was once the league's head of innovation," Elliot muttered. "Worked on live stat integration. Moved sideways. Quiet, private. No enemies."

"Now he's the leak," Tash said flatly.

They found Kreel not in his office, but at a mental wellness seminar the AFL had discreetly funded for senior staff. A soft name. A safe space. "Work-Life Resilience in Modern Sport."

He looked older than his 47 years. Slumped posture. Skin sallow. Like something inside him had been rotting for years.

"I know why you're here," he said before they sat.

"We're not journalists," Elliot said.

"Good," Kreel replied. "Because I can't survive another headline."

He handed over a flash drive. "This is what I accessed. Not to sell. Not to leak. I downloaded it because I wanted to see."

"See what?" Tash asked.

"If it was true. If the system I built was being used to lie."

"And was it?" Elliot asked.

Kreel didn't answer.

He just stared past them, toward the floor-to-ceiling window.

"They told me the algorithm was for transparency. That it would 'protect' vote secrecy and track unauthorized access. But then they installed a backdoor. One only a handful of execs could use."

He looked down at his trembling hands.

"After I saw what they were doing… I stopped sleeping. I stopped speaking to my kids. I started seeing the game differently. Not as a competition — but a screenplay. And I was the technician backstage, cueing the lights."

Tash placed her hand gently on the table.

"Daniel. You're not the only one."

"But I might be the only one who saw it before it happened," he whispered. "I saw them shaping the count. I watched the edits. And I did… nothing."

Elliot's voice softened.

"You did something now."

Kreel laughed bitterly.

"They'll know I spoke to you. They track every drive. Every keystroke. The moment you plug that in, my name lights up."

"So tell us more," Tash said. "Before we even open it."

He nodded slowly.

"They changed the votes," he said. "Not always dramatically — just enough. A 3 becomes a 2. A 2 becomes silence. It was done in a room with five people. Always the same ones. They call it alignment. 'Aligning the count with the narrative.'"

"Names?" Elliot asked.

Kreel shook his head. "If I say them, I disappear."

"You've already put your name on the drive."

"I know."

He stood. His hands trembled more now.

"I just wanted to build something honest," he said. "Something that would let players trust the system again."

He turned away.

Then stopped.

"You ever wonder why the Brownlow's always at Crown?"

Elliot blinked. "What?"

"It's not just logistics. Crown hosts the betting markets. The suites. The rooms where real votes are tallied. Sometimes... the casino knows before the umpires do."

Then he walked out.

And Elliot felt something new settle over him.

Not anger. Not even grief.

Dread.

CHAPTER 15

The House Always Knows

The Crown complex gleamed like a polished blade in the Melbourne night. Neon reflections rippled in the Yarra River as gamblers drifted through sliding glass doors, unaware—or unwilling to care—that the building was more than a casino.

It was a cathedral to perception.

Elliot stood across the road with Tash, staring up at the windows of Level 27 — the "private function" floor, where the Brownlow votes were counted and sealed behind security, champagne, and smiles.

"It's not just a count," Tash said. "It's a performance."

"And the audience never asks who wrote the script."

Inside, they weren't invited — but they weren't exactly strangers either. Elliot still had contacts in the event coordination team, and Tash had looped a dormant access badge ID through the RFID system via a courier database.

They dressed in black. No names. No questions.

Level 27 was quiet. No security posted until three days before the actual event. The suite was empty except for polished chairs, digital projection gear, and a lockbox built into the back wall, disguised as a wine cabinet.

Tash picked it.

Inside: paperwork. Brownlow count templates. Draft graphic slides. Printouts marked "Partner Brief – Gaming Integrations."

And then… the list.

The real count — votes from previous years, tallied before the broadcast, with side columns listing betting odds before and after the results went public.

"What is this?" Elliot muttered.

Tash's face was drained. "A betting schema."

The AFL and Crown weren't just partners — they were co-authors. The votes weren't only for awards — they were for markets. Each player's polling pattern matched market fluctuations down to the minute.

"You could bet in play during the count," Tash whispered. "And they knew the right time to surge a player's odds… or crash them."

A noise.

Elliot turned. Down the hallway, a man stood watching them.

Middle-aged. Suit. Calm.

Not security. Worse.

Milo Venner — Head of Strategic Wagering Partnerships for Crown. Former sports agent. Long-time AFL "friend."

He stepped into the light.

"You two have gone too far," he said.

"No," Elliot said, stepping forward. "We've gone deep enough."

Venner smiled thinly.

"You think anyone will believe you? We're not hiding this. We're hosting it. Crown has naming rights. AFL gets its integrity tick. The betting agencies get their margins. Everyone eats."

"Except the players," Tash snapped.

"Oh, they eat too. You think Colville's Nike deal came from clean hands?"

Venner stepped closer.

"This isn't corruption," he said coldly. "It's capitalism. Don't confuse the two."

Elliot's fists clenched. "You rigged a sacred thing."

Venner smiled. "We repackaged it. Made it profitable. Palatable. Playable. You want justice? There's no market for that."

Tash took one final photo of the documents.

And Venner let them go.

Because he didn't believe in fear anymore.

That was the worst part.

As they exited, Elliot said nothing. The cold night bit into his skin like guilt.

"Why didn't he stop us?" Tash asked softly.

Elliot stared out at the river.

"Because he doesn't think he has to."

The Winner's Burden

His name was Isaac "Zac" Colville — midfielder, fan-favourite, dual club champion, and this year's Brownlow frontrunner. Tysons younger brother.

He called Elliot anonymously. A burner number. No caller ID.

"I need to talk," the voice said.

They met after midnight in a gym near Port Melbourne — one Colville part-owned but never promoted. A warehouse shell with free weights, scuffed leather benches, and silence that echoed.

Zac stood in track pants, hoodie up, arms folded like a man waiting for judgment. He looked lean. Lighter than his playing weight. His eyes darted to the corners of the room.

"You're not recording this?" he asked.

"No," Elliot said.

Tash stayed back. She knew when to let a man speak his own guilt.

Zac paced before starting.

"I'm going to win the Brownlow."

"Congratulations," Elliot said, dry.

Zac stopped. "That's the problem. I know I'm going to win. They told me."

Elliot's spine straightened.

"Who?"

"My manager. His contact at the league. Said I should start preparing my speech. Said it was 'part of the bigger picture.'"

Elliot stayed silent.

Zac continued.

"Last year I finished fifth. This year I've been good… but not that good. Couple of standout games. A few media hits. A sponsor boost. Then… the votes started following me like shadows."

He sat on the bench, hands between his knees.

"You want to know the worst part? I played better the year I didn't poll. Now… I'm being crowned for a version of me I don't recognize. One built on branding, not effort."

Tash finally stepped forward.

"Why come forward now?"

Zac looked at her. His voice cracked.

"Because I can't tell my old man. He's been to every game since under-12s. Tells everyone the Brownlow's the 'fairest and best.' He believed that."

He turned to Elliot.

"Do you know what it feels like to be rewarded for a lie? To watch your teammates kill themselves for a contest that was pre-decided?"

"I do," Elliot said softly.

Zac leaned back.

"I want out. I don't want the medal. But if I say anything, I'm ruined. Sponsorships, career, legacy. I'll be called bitter. Jealous. Mental."

"Then give us your story," Tash said. "Not for the cameras. For the record."

Zac looked at them both, then nodded once.

"I'll do it. On one condition."

"What?"

"If something happens to me… tell the world everything."

As they left, Elliot looked over his shoulder.

Zac stayed behind, sitting in silence, as if he were already rehearsing a speech he didn't believe in — or mourning the player he used to be.

Outside, Tash whispered: "Even the winner wants out."

Elliot didn't reply.

Because some truths don't need repeating.

They just need telling.

CHAPTER 17

Silence in the Noise

The story dropped on a Tuesday.

Front page. Prime-time bulletin. Headlines everywhere.

"Brownlow Compromised? Leaked Data Suggests Vote Manipulation, Insider Betting"

The journalist was Gerry O'Sullivan — old-school, feared, and meticulous. Tash fed him just enough to verify, cross-check, and publish with fireproof legal backing. Gerry had been sitting on stories like this for years. But no one had dared go public.

Until now.

The article detailed:

Leaked voting drafts showing pre-count manipulation.

Ties between vote changes and betting markets.

Crown's suspected prior knowledge of outcomes.

A quiet pattern of media conditioning favouring selects players.

The sudden death of Cleo Watson — and a whistleblower now missing.

It was all there. Names redacted. Sources protected. But the truth unmistakable.

And the public reaction?

Muted.

Confused.

Defensive.

Social media exploded — not with outrage, but uncertainty.

> "Fake news."
> "Jealous ex-player."
> "Everyone bets — get over it."
> "The AFL would never risk the Brownlow."
> "You just hate footy."

Elliot read each comment like a wound reopening. Tash was quieter than usual, her hands still but her eyes electric.

"We gave them truth," she said finally. "And they chose denial."

"They're not ready," Elliot replied. "We just told them the game they grew up worshipping is rigged. That their heroes are mannequins. People don't wake up from that gently."

Then came the AFL's response.

A short statement. Measured. Legal.

> "We categorically deny any wrongdoing in the administration of the Brownlow Medal. We are deeply committed to the integrity of the game. An internal review is underway."

That was it.

No press conference. No outrage. No suspensions.

Just… silence.

And in the silence, fear spread.

Former players didn't call.

Current players avoided social media.

Sponsors kept buying airtime like nothing had changed.

It was like yelling fire in a theatre and watching everyone keep eating their popcorn.

Tash stared at the screen, numb.

"Maybe they're afraid," she said. "Not just of us. But of knowing. Because if they admit it's true… they'd have to admit what they've been cheering for."

Elliot nodded.

"The scariest truth," he said, "is the one that demands you change."

Outside, the world went on. Match previews rolled out. Pundits picked favourites. Crown reopened their Brownlow betting market by noon.

As if nothing had happened.

As if truth was the most forgettable story of the week.

CHAPTER 18

The Long Night

It was past midnight when Elliot's phone buzzed.

A name flashed he hadn't seen in years: Dylan Morley.

Ex-teammate. Best and fairest runner-up. Life member at Carlton. Quiet. Reliable. The kind of man who never made headlines — except once, five years ago, when his younger brother Nathan, a club staffer, died by suicide.

The coroner's report had ruled it without suspicion.

The club said it was "tragic."

Dylan never spoke publicly again.

Now he wanted to meet.

They sat in a parked car outside a rundown sports complex in Preston. No one else around. Dylan hadn't aged well. Eyes sunken. Shoulders tight.

"I've been watching," Dylan said. "The stories. The fallout. What you're chasing."

Elliot nodded. "Then you know what I'm going to ask."

Dylan pulled a crumpled photo from his coat. Four men, blurry, mid-conversation. A familiar face among them: a current club CEO — now seen shaking hands with known mob affiliates.

"My brother Nathan was a data analyst for the club," Dylan said. "He flagged inconsistencies in vote stats. Not just polling — performance metrics. Said they didn't match game-day footage. That they were being 'cleaned.'"

Elliot's blood chilled.

"Cleaned by who?"

"Not sure. But two weeks later, he was pulled into a 'welfare meeting.' After that, he stopped talking. I found a draft message on his laptop. He never sent it."

He passed Elliot a folded paper. It read:

> "I don't know who to trust. The votes don't
> match the data. The system's infected —
> not just votes. Money. Agents. CEO's office.
> If something happens to me, start there."

Elliot looked up. "Why now, Dylan?"

Dylan's eyes glossed.

"Because I've been a coward. Because I watched you go first."

He left quietly. No handshake. Just a nod.

Later, in the dark quiet of Tash's apartment, Elliot sat at her kitchen bench, staring at the message.

She approached with tea, setting it beside him.

He didn't speak.

Then: "Do you ever wonder if we're making it worse?"

Tash paused. "What do you mean?"

"People dying. People backing away. And the public? They look right through it. Like the truth's too ugly to digest."

Tash leaned against the bench.

"I think that's why it needs to be told. Because most people don't know how to look. But they'll remember when someone finally shows them."

He looked up at her — really looked.

The fatigue in her shoulders, the defiance in her jawline. She was the strongest person he'd met in years. And he didn't even know what she was sacrificing to stay in the fight.

"Tash…" he began.

But stopped.

She held his gaze. "What?"

He swallowed.

"I'm scared too."

She didn't move. Just stepped closer.

And then — quiet, without rush or explanation — she rested her forehead gently against his.

No kiss. No grand gesture. Just contact.

Just warmth in a cold world.

Just enough to remind them both they weren't alone.

CHAPTER 19

Blood in the Water

The summons arrived at dawn.

A thick envelope hand-delivered by a private courier. No knock. No eye contact. Just left on the doorstep.

"Statement of Claim — Defamation and Unauthorized Possession of Protected AFL Materials."

Tash read it twice. Elliot only once.

"This isn't a warning," she said. "This is a missile."

They were being sued — jointly and separately — by the AFL, under a battery of charges ranging from digital intrusion to reputational damage. The papers named Elliot specifically.

"A disgruntled former player with a history of inflammatory conduct."

It was a character assassination wrapped in legal ink.

An emergency press conference was held by the AFL's Head of Integrity, who looked straight down the barrel of the camera and called the reporting "a dangerous conspiracy orchestrated by people with personal grudges and distorted memories."

They never said Elliot's name.

But the footy world heard it loud and clear.

By noon, every radio station had queued up his old suspensions, his turbulent exit, his final season "disappearance." TV panels speculated about "mental health breakdowns" and "long-standing beef with the league." Former teammates distanced themselves.

Sponsors dropped him. A podcast deal vanished.

The same public that shrugged at corruption now found its target — and turned with a hunger.

Tash stormed into the apartment, throwing her phone onto the couch.

"They're winning the perception war."

"They always did," Elliot said.

She stared at him.

"Then fight back."

He hesitated.

She saw it.

"What are you hiding?" she asked gently.

He took a long breath.

"There was a game. My last year. Round 14. I was told — not asked — told by a club exec to take a certain player out of the game. Not dirty, just physical. Intimidate. Distract."

"And?"

"I did."

He closed his eyes.

"The kid went down in the third quarter. Broken collarbone. Missed the rest of the season. He was leading our club's Brownlow votes at the time."

Tash stood in stunned silence.

"I thought I was just being a team man. But later I realised… it wasn't about the game. It was about the count. They removed him. And used me to do it."

"And you never said anything?"

"I buried it. Told myself it was part of footy. But now…"

He opened the bottom drawer of the cabinet and pulled out a sealed envelope — old, worn, unopened.

"It's a letter. From him. The kid I hit. He sent it years later. I never opened it."

Tash looked at him.

"Do it now."

His fingers shook as he tore the flap.

Inside, a single line:

"I forgive you. But one day, tell the truth."

Elliot sat in silence.

Tash sat beside him.

"Then let's tell it," She said softly. "All of it. Starting with this."

And for the first time since the suit was filed, Elliot smiled.

Not with triumph.

But with peace.

The Bloodhound's Bark

The AFL's legal counsel expected a quick dismissal. A procedural win. A shut-it-down special.

They didn't expect Brad Hardie.

The tribunal chamber was packed — media, club representatives, legal observers. Elliot and Tash sat quietly, front row, beneath fluorescent lights that buzzed louder than the chatter.

Brad entered mid-hearing.

No lawyer.

Just a battered leather satchel, a worn notepad, and the presence of someone who'd been underestimated most of his life.

He wasn't on the witness list.

But he wasn't here for permission.

"Mr. Hardie," the lead adjudicator said with surprise, "you are not formally attached to this proceeding."

Brad grinned. "No, but I reckon truth doesn't always wait for invitations."

A murmur.

He stood and addressed the room like a man who'd called a thousand games — and saw through every one of them.

"I've been covering this game for 40 years. Played it. Bled for it. And I've watched it become something else — something manufactured."

He held up a sheaf of printed betting slips.

"These are wagers placed before last year's Brownlow count. Same names. Same exact vote margins. Same corporate suite ticket holders."

The tribunal chair tried to interrupt.

Brad rolled on.

"I've spoken to four retired umpires — off the record. All say they were subtly influenced before key matches. None were paid. But they were pressured. Rewarded with finals gigs if they kept the narrative neat."

He turned to Elliot.

"This man's not bitter. He's brave. He's saying what everyone in the back bar's whispered for years."

Then he pointed at the AFL counsel table.

"And you lot — you know it. You just hope no one listens."

Silence.

A silence filled with power.

The media exploded as Brad walked out — no statement, no press conference. Just a nod to Elliot and a hand on his shoulder.

"Don't stop now," he said. "You're not alone anymore."

Outside, the tide shifted.

Commentators who'd stayed neutral started asking questions. A former Brownlow medallist tweeted support. Sponsors paused their auto-renewals. AFL executives ducked interviews.

And behind closed doors, a whisper ran through the system:

"The truth's leaking. And no one can plug it."

That night, Elliot and Tash stood on her balcony, watching the city lights flicker like nervous blinks.

"They're scrambling," she said.

"They should be," Elliot replied. "Because next..."

He held up the file Ronnie Tilton had given them.

"...we name names."

CHAPTER 21

The Count Ends Here

They held the press conference in the back room of an old community footy club — the kind with peeling paint, torn honour boards, and soul.

Elliot wore no tie. Tash ran the AV.

It wasn't about spectacle. It was about truth.

On the screen behind him: the names.

Executives. Club CEOs. Data officials. Two agents. And most damning — one current umpire still on the AFL's roster.

Beside each name: evidence. Vote alteration logs. Bet traces. Internal emails. Instructions disguised as "matchday briefing summaries."

Then came the recording.

Cleo's final voice memo, cleaned up for clarity.

"This isn't a sport anymore. It's a market dressed as a memory. The Brownlow isn't the fairest and best — it's the most convenient. And I think they know I know."

You could hear the room inhale.

When Elliot stepped to the mic, the flashbulbs started. He let them pop. Then raised a hand.

"I grew up loving this game. I still do. But love isn't silence. Love tells the truth, even when it hurts."

He paused.

"Every name behind me chose money over meaning. Image over honesty. Some of them still think they're safe — because the public doesn't want the truth."

A beat.

"Then maybe it's time the public grew up."

He closed with a sentence that would run on every back page in the country:

> "If this is the cost of telling the truth… I'll
> pay it."

The aftermath came fast.

The AFL issued an emergency statement denying "any systemic wrongdoing," but vowed to "cooperate with investigations."

Three executives resigned within 72 hours.

The umpire was quietly removed from the finals panel.

Crown's AFL betting arm was suspended pending review.

A Senate inquiry into sports integrity was opened.

Zac Colville returned his Brownlow medal before the ceremony, releasing a single line: "I want to be remembered for how I played, not for how I was picked."

And Elliot?

He became the reluctant face of the biggest sporting scandal in modern Australian history.

Epilogue

The following season began like they all do — with fresh boots, new recruits, and hopeful headlines.

But the count?

The Brownlow was suspended for the first time since World War II.

In its place: silence.

And in that silence, a question echoed through the country:

> "What do we cheer for when the game isn't fair?"

Elliot watched the opening round from a quiet pub in Fremantle. Tash sat beside him. No cameras. No speeches.

Just footy.

Real footy.

And for the first time in a long time — it felt honest again.

THE END

Disclaimer

This is a work of fiction.

Names, characters, businesses, organizations, events, and incidents are either the product of the author's imagination or used in a fictional manner. Any resemblance to actual persons, living or dead, or actual events, organizations, or sporting bodies — including but not limited to the AFL, Crown Casino, or any individual player, umpire, or executive — is purely coincidental.

The narrative is intended to explore themes of integrity, truth, and power within the broader context of professional sport. It is not a commentary on any specific league, organization, or individual.

No real-world allegations are being made, nor should any part of this book be interpreted as fact.

9 781968 667030